ALISON HUGHES   NINON PELLETIER

The Silence Slips In

ORCA BOOK PUBLISHERS

The Silence is shy and soft. Shaggy and still.

It peers around corners and waits quietly,
ready to soothe and smooth the sharp,
jagged edges left by the Noise.

When the others have chattered and shrieked their way home, when the balloons have all popped, when the baby finally falls asleep, when the dog is all barked out, and the screens are dark the Silence slips in.

It appears slowly, like a watery rainbow
after a storm, after the Noise's tantrum of
thunder and rain has rolled on.

It watches the snow fall in the early
morning and curls up in a sunbeam with
a warm, cuddly cat.

The Silence loves reading. Thinking.
Long hugs. And mugs of hot chocolate
by a peaceful fire.

The Silence slips in at bedtime and greets
its friend the Dark. They bring warm,
soft blankets and settle in.

The Silence holds you in its safe, soothing
arms and lulls you to sleep. And gently,
softly launches all the boats of your dreams.

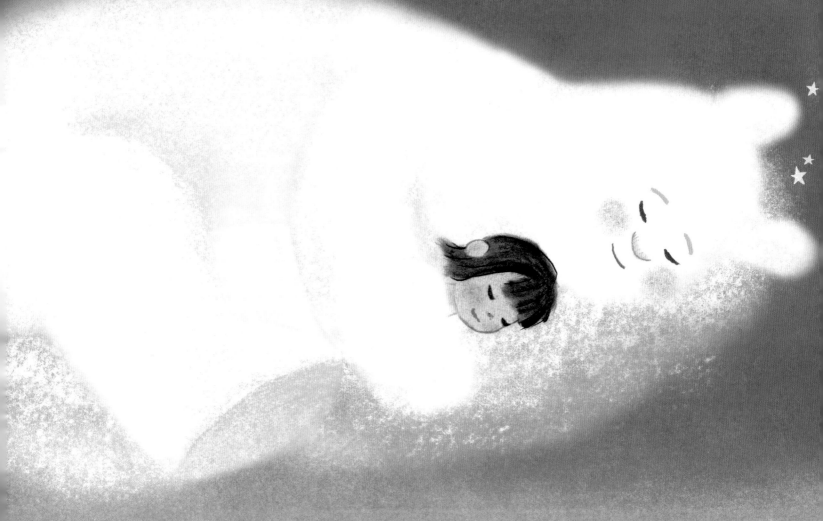

In the morning, when the birds start to sing and the baby wakes up, the Noise hammers on the door and clatters back in. And the Silence slips away.

Back to its home in a quiet room.
A peaceful garden. The forest. The
mountains. The ocean. Or the deep,
deep sky.

But the Silence will come back whenever you call it. Whenever you need it. Even in the midst of the Noise and its ruckus.

If you close your eyes and breathe deeply, the Silence will pad in on its soft, furry feet and surround you.

Your busy mind will settle. And you
will smile a peaceful little smile.

As the Silence slips in.

For Kate, Ben and Sam—may you always find your own Silence —A.H.

To my mother —N.P.

Text copyright © 2019 Alison Hughes
Illustrations copyright © 2019 Ninon Pelletier

Cataloguing in Publication information available from Library and Archives Canada

Issued in print and electronic formats.
ISBN 978-1-4598-1706-7 (hardcover).— ISBN 978-1-4598-1707-4 (pdf).—
ISBN 978-1-4598-1708-1 (epub)

Also available as *Le Silence se glisse près de toi*, a French-language picture book (ISBN 978-1-4598-2208-5)

Simultaneously published in Canada and the United States in 2019
Library of Congress Control Number: 2018954103

Summary: In this illustrated picture book, a young child learns to find comfort in silence when the world becomes too noisy.

Orca Book Publishers is dedicated to preserving the environment and has printed this book on Forest Stewardship Council® certified paper and other controlled materials.

Orca Book Publishers gratefully acknowledges the support for its publishing programs provided by the following agencies: the Government of Canada, the Canada Council for the Arts and the Province of British Columbia through the BC Arts Council and the Book Publishing Tax Credit.

Artwork created in pencil and charcoal and digitally colored.
Cover and interior artwork by Ninon Pelletier
Edited by Liz Kemp
Design by Rachel Page

ORCA BOOK PUBLISHERS
orcabook.com

Printed and bound in China.

22 21 20 19 • 4 3 2 1

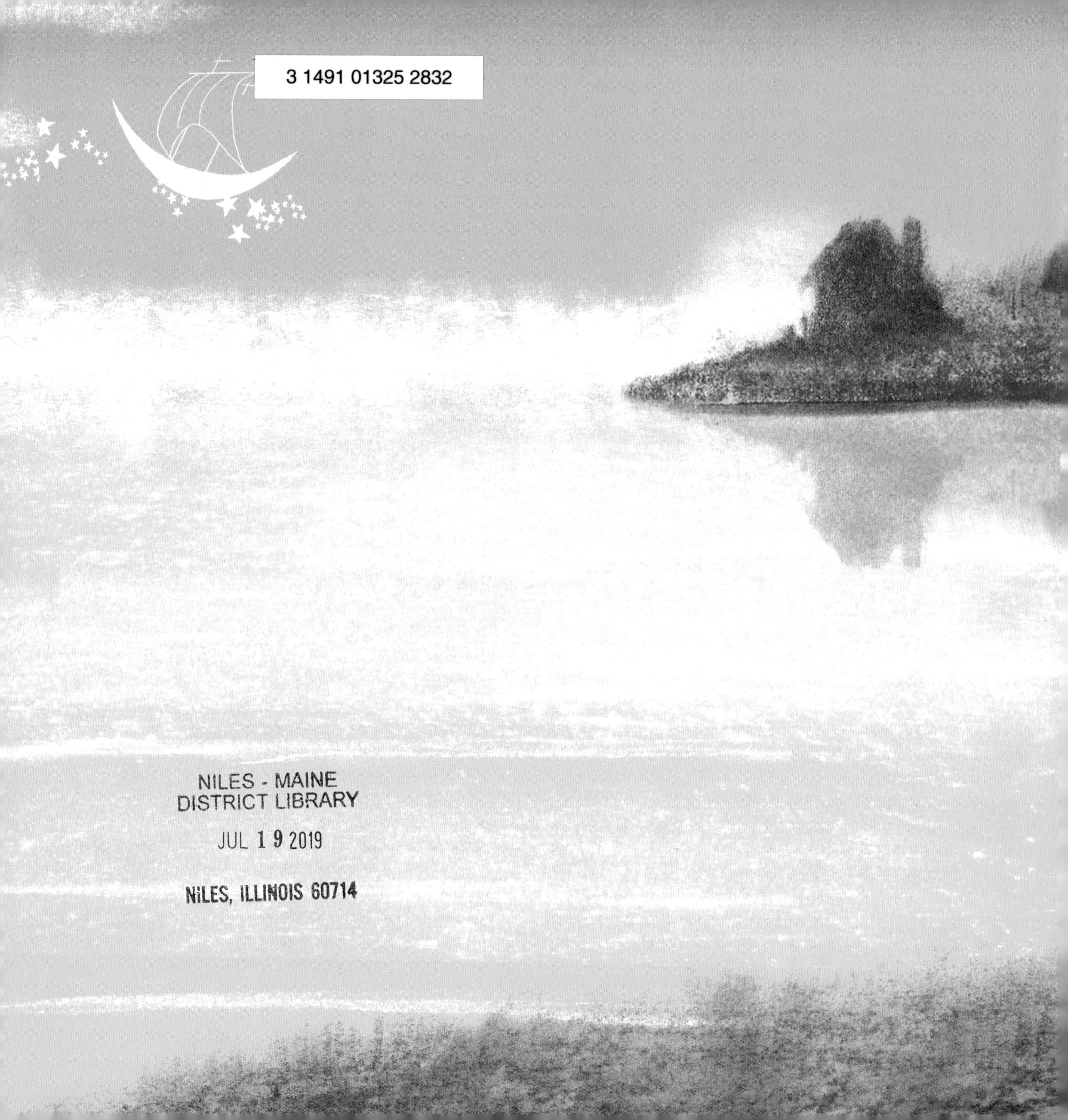